TEDDY
and
The Mystery of The Missing Milk

"All is not well," Teddy heard them all say.
"Some more milk was taken only yesterday.
Teddy Milkbear left it by the front door,
But when Mrs. Bruin looked, it was there no more."

''It's a mystery,'' they said, ''it happens every day,
Who can it be that steals the milk away?''
Teddy and his friends listened to the talk,
And then quietly decided to go for a walk.

''It's a mystery,'' they said, ''it happens every day,
Who can it be that steals the milk away?''

Bessy Bear said, ''It's happened before,
    Only last week it disappeared from our door.''
''It is very mysterious,'' Jimbo said.
    ''Who takes the milk,
When we're all snug in bed?''

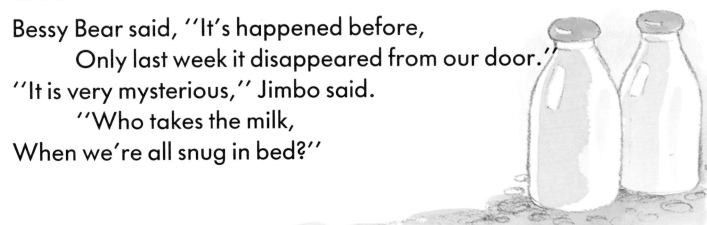

Teddy Bear said, with a solemn frown,
   "We must catch this thief of infamous renown."
"Those are big words," Jimbo declared.
   "But catch him we will, we're not scared."

Teddy Bear said, ''We must plan very hard,
        And catch the thief when he's off his guard.
Tomorrow morning, before the cock crows,
        We will get up early and see if he shows.''

Jimbo said, ''Let's meet at six,
        And like real detectives, carry walking sticks.
A walking stick is a jolly good idea,
        A magnifying glass also, will make things clear.''

As the church clock chimed six,
 The Detective Bears met.
The sun was just rising,
 And the grass was dew wet.
''Milkbear has already
 Started his round,
So let's keep our eyes peeled
 Close to the ground.''

Teddy Bear led them down the village street,
But stopped to examine some marks by a seat.
"Our thief has small feet," he said with a frown,
Just then came a shout from Mister Bear Brown.

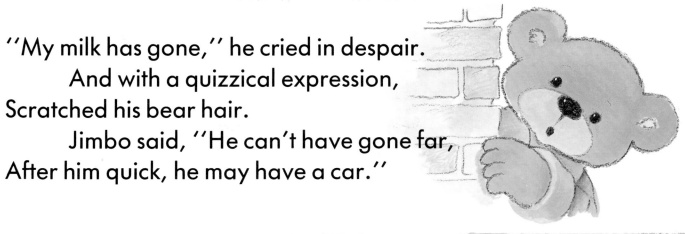

"My milk has gone," he cried in despair.
And with a quizzical expression,
Scratched his bear hair.
Jimbo said, "He can't have gone far,
After him quick, he may have a car."

Up and down the street they looked in vain,
     But their eyes saw nothing, so they all looked again.
"This thief is crafty," Teddy Bear said.
     "He may have small feet, but he's one step ahead!"

''Let's examine the facts,'' Teddy Bear said,
   ''The thief must have struck when we were in bed.
Tomorrow at five, we all must meet,
   Then perhaps we can stop him having his treat.''

At five the next morning,
    By the village green,
They looked all around,
    But not a soul could be seen.
Milkbear had started,
    Already that day,
And the bears followed on,
    A short distance away.

Suddenly from behind, a cry was heard,
    ''Who's taken my milk?''
''Not me!'' said a bird.
    A cheeky sparrow was perched in a tree,
''Call yourselves detectives?
    You couldn't catch a flea!''

Just then, Post Bear appeared delivering the mail,
        ''I think your thief might have a bushy tail.''
The bears asked him just what he had seen.
        With a smile, he pointed across the village green.

"Behind Grandma Bear's cottage,
    There's a cat, smooth as silk.
And I saw her this morning,
    With a bottle of milk."
The bears scampered to the cottage,
    Behind which was a shed,
And inside saw six kittens,
    All tucked up in bed.

Mother Cat was feeding them, in bed where they lay,
Tiny and snug in the sweet smelling hay.
When she first saw the bears,
She was startled at the sight,
But then told them all of her sad, sorry plight.

The kittens had been poorly,
    And needed extra food.
She knew stealing was wrong,
    But hoped they understood.
As soon as they were strong,
    They would start to repay.
By chasing all the village mice, far, far away.

The bears were happy to hear,
    What Mother Cat had to tell,
And told her not to worry,
    And that all would soon be well.
They would ask Milkbear to deliver,
    A special pint for her,
And send a 'GET WELL SOON' card,
    For the cats with silken fur.

So all has ended happily,
    The kittens are fit and well.
I hope you enjoyed this story,
    It was a tale I had to tell!